by John Thomas

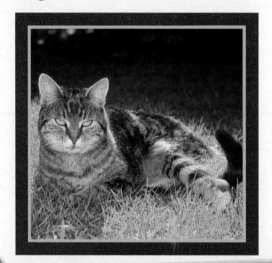

Strategy Focus

Read each page, and think about what the cat might do next.

HOUGHTON MIFFLIN   BOSTON

Story Vocabulary

cat

go

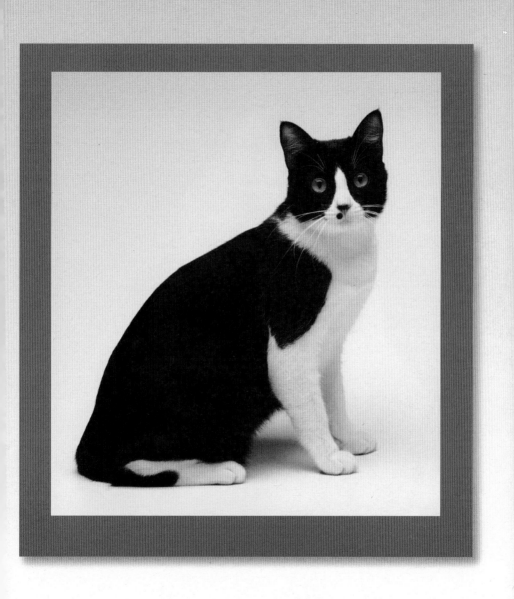

I see the cat.

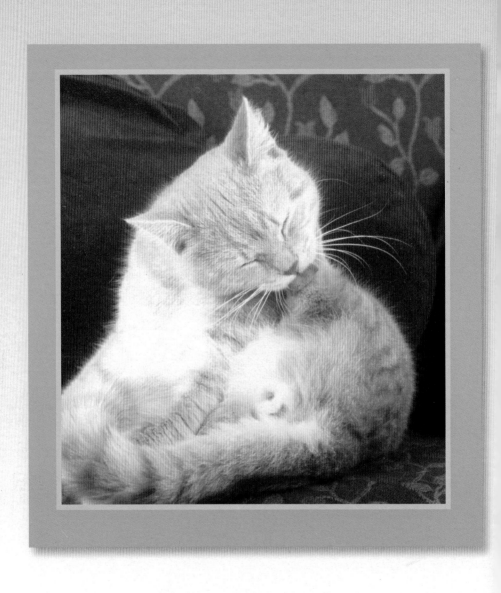

I see the cat.

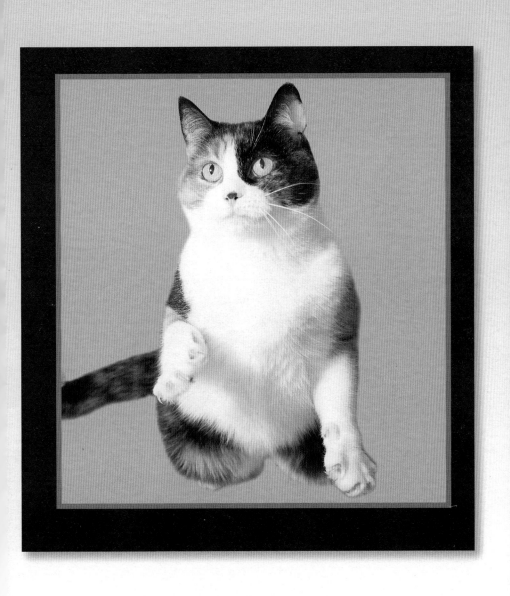

I see the cat.

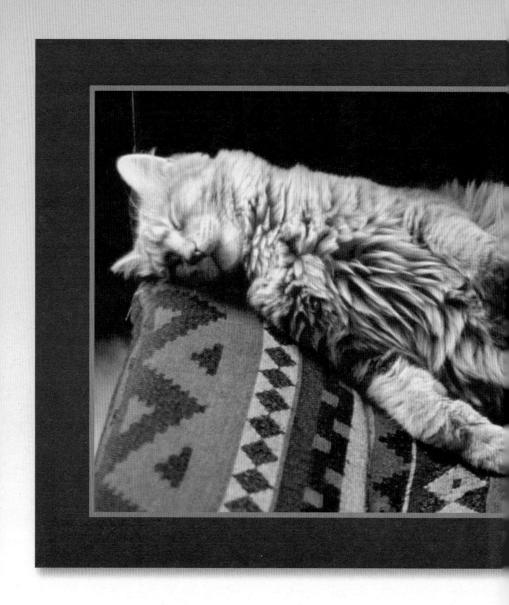

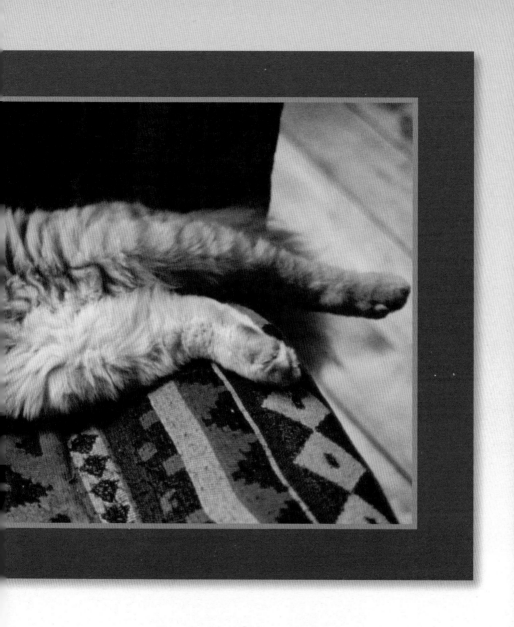

I see the cat.

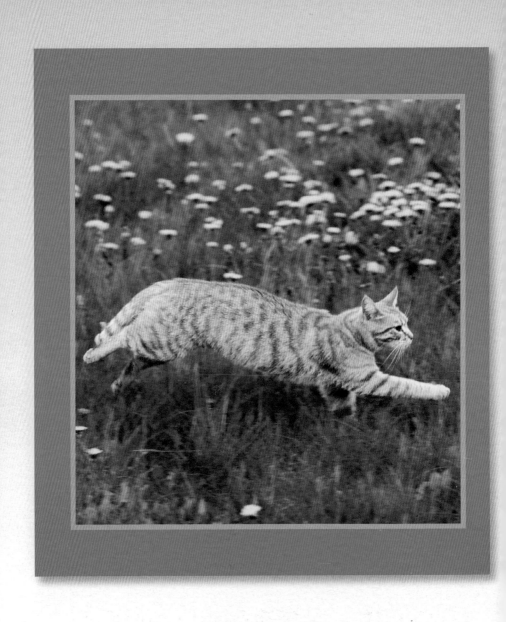

Go, cat!